Printed and Bound in April 2013 at Tien Wah Press, Johor Bahru, Johor, Malaysia.
The text typeface is Report School.
The artwork was created with pen and ink and watercolors.
www.holidayhouse.com
First Edition
1 3 5 7 9 10 8 6 4 2

Library of Congress Cataloging-in-Publication Data
McCully, Emily Arnold.
Pete won't eat / by Emily Arnold McCully. — 1st ed.
p. cm. — (I like to read)
Summary: Pete the pig does not want to eat his slop, but cannot go
out to play with his brother and sisters until he does.
ISBN 978-0-8234-2853-3 (hardcover)
[1. Food habits—Fiction. 2. Pigs—Fiction.] I. Title. II. Title: Pete will not eat.
PZ7.M478415Pet 2013
[E]—dc23
2012039209

Pete Won't Eat

by

Emily Arnold McCully

Holiday House / New York

"I made a treat,"
says Mom.

"Here it is—green slop."

Dot loves the slop.

Rose slurps the slop.

Gus has all of it.

But Pete won't eat.

“Slop is good,” says Mom.
“No,” says Pete.

“Try one bite,”
says Mom.
“No,” says Pete.

"Eat your slop," say Dot, Rose, and Gus. "We want to go out and play."
"I won't!" says Pete.

“Dot, Rose, and Gus
may go,” says Mom.
“I hate green,”
says Pete.

“Bye,” says Dot.
“We will be in the yard,”
says Rose.

“You will stay until you eat,”
says Mom.

“I hope he tries it,”
says Mom.

"Yuck," says Pete.

"I want
to go out,"
says Pete.
"I want
to play."

"It's getting late,"
says Mom.

The kids call.
"Come out
and play."

"Please eat your slop, Pete,"
says Mom.

“I hate green slop,”
says Pete. “Poor me.”

Mom cries.
“I am a mean mom!”

“I will make something Pete likes.”

“I will make you a sandwich,”
says Mom.

Pete looks at the slop.
"How **does** it taste?"
says Pete.

"It's not bad."

"It's good!"
says Pete.

Mom sees Pete eat.
"No need for this,"
she says.

Now Pete can go out.
"Here I am!" says Pete.
"Let's play!"

The next day,
Pete and Mom
make more slop.

I Like to Read® Books

You will like all of them!

Boy, Bird, and Dog by David McPhail
Car Goes Far by Michael Garland
Come Back, Ben by Ann Hassett and John Hassett
Dinosaurs Don't, Dinosaurs Do by Steve Björkman
Fireman Fred by Lynn Rowe Reed
Fish Had a Wish by Michael Garland
The Fly Flew In by David Catrow
Happy Cat by Steve Henry
I Have a Garden by Bob Barner
I Will Try by Marilyn Janovitz
Late Nate in a Race by Emily Arnold McCully
The Lion and the Mice
by Rebecca Emberley and Ed Emberley
Look! by Ted Lewin
Me Too! by Valeri Gorbachev
Mice on Ice
by Rebecca Emberley and Ed Emberley
Pete Won't Eat by Emily Arnold McCully
Pig Has a Plan by Ethan Long
Sam and the Big Kids by Emily Arnold McCully
See Me Dig by Paul Meisel
See Me Run by Paul Meisel
A Theodor Seuss Geisel Award Honor Book
Sick Day by David McPhail
What Am I? Where Am I? by Ted Lewin
You Can Do It! by Betsy Lewin